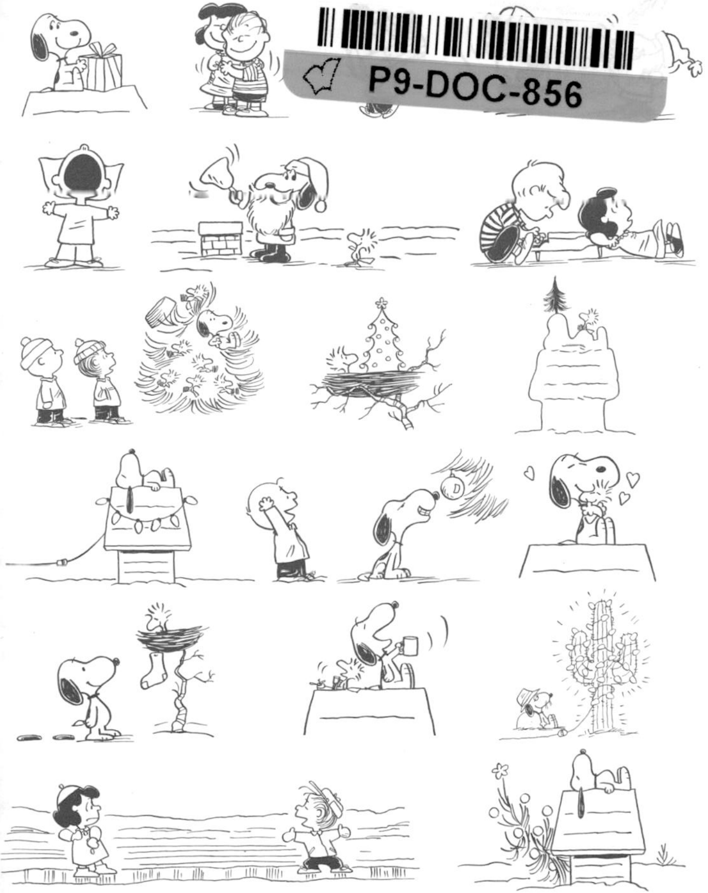

Be
JOYFUL

PEANUTS WISDOM TO CARRY YOU THROUGH

Published by Running Press,
A Member of the Perseus Books Group

Printed in China

Books published by Running Press are available at special discounts for bulk purchases in the United States by corporations, institutions, and other organizations. For more information, please contact the Special Markets Department at the Perseus Books Group, 2300 Chestnut Street, Suite 200, Philadelphia, PA 19103, or call (800) 810-4145, ext. 5000, or e-mail special.markets@perseusbooks.com.

ISBN 978-0-7624-4719 0
Library of Congress Control Number: 2014935444

9 8 7 6 5 4 3 2 1
Digit on the right indicates the number of this printing

Artwork created by Charles M. Schulz
For Charles M. Schulz Creative Associates: pencils by Vicki Scott,
inks by Paige Braddock, colors by Alexis E. Fajardo
Designed by T.L. Bonaddio
Edited by Marlo Scrimizzi
Typography: Archer, Clarendon, Duality, Gill Sans, Banda, Emmascript, Kabel

Running Press Book Publishers
2300 Chestnut Street
Philadelphia, PA 19103-4371

Visit us on the web!
www.runningpress.com
www.snoopy.com

Be
JOYFUL

PEANUTS WISDOM TO CARRY YOU THROUGH

Based on the comic strip, PEANUTS,
by Charles M. Schulz

Running PRESS
PHILADELPHIA · LONDON

"Christmas is doing a
little something extra
for someone."

—*Charles M. Schulz*

Be
CHEERY

Lucy: Somehow I feel that I have more of the real spirit of Christmas this year than ever before!

Linus: Why do you suppose that is?

Lucy: Because I said so, that's why!

Be
patient

Charlie Brown: A package just came for you, but it says, "Do not open until Christmas."

Snoopy: Dogs can't read! Hee, hee, hee!

Be EXCITED

"Merry Christmas, old friend. Whee! Whoopee!
Wow! Right on!"

—*Snoopy*

Be
APPRECIATIVE

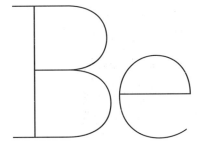

"Anyone who would fly around from house to house in a sleigh with a bunch of reindeer, at night yet, has to be out of his mind! But we appreciate it!"

—*Snoopy*

Be
GOOD

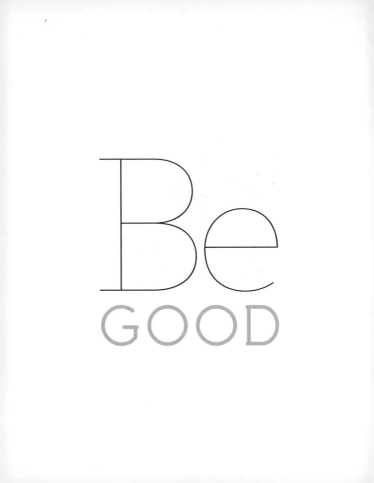

Lucy: Are you sending those greedy letters to Santa Claus again?

Linus: I'm not greedy! All I want is what I have coming to me. All I want is my fair share!

Lucy: Santa Claus doesn't owe you anything!

Linus: He does if I've been good! That's the agreement! Any tenth-grade student of commercial law could tell you that!

Be
Mesmerized

Be
DECKED

Be OPTIMISTIC

"My dog is back! He's back! Oh, it's going to be a Merry Christmas after all."

—*Charlie Brown*

Be
COMRADES

Lucy: Merry Christmas, Charlie Brown! At this time of year I think we should put aside all our differences and try to be kind.

Charlie Brown: Why does it have to be for just this time of year? Why can't it be all year round?

Lucy: What are you, some kind of fanatic or something?

Be

Adorning

"I love tall trees!"

—*Snoopy*

Be

MELODIOUS

Sally: I wish I could do something to cheer you up. . . .

Charlie Brown: Please don't sing Christmas carols!

Be
DELIGHTED

"I love the holiday season!"

—*Snoopy*

Be
Electric

Be
POSITIVE

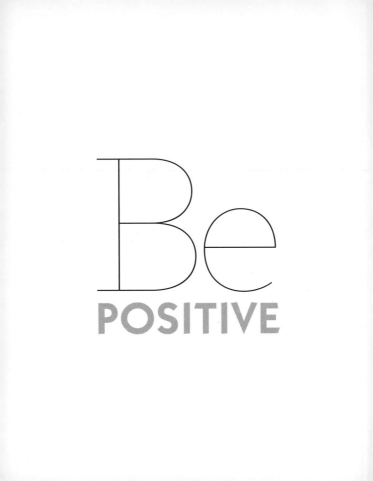

Charlie Brown: Christmas is over, but I still feel joyful. I think I'm going to be able to keep this good feeling about myself and everyone for a real long time.

Lucy: Who cares?

Be
EXUBERANT

"Season's greetings."

—*Snoopy*

Be
UPBEAT

Charlie Brown: Christmas Eve is my favorite day of the year. It makes me feel good about everything. I wish I could put it into words. . . .

Snoopy: My aerobics class was cancelled.

Be
Kind

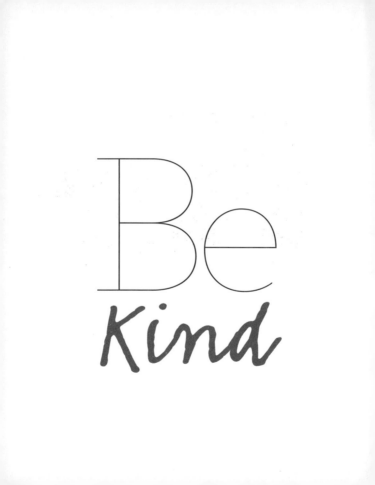

Be
ICONIC

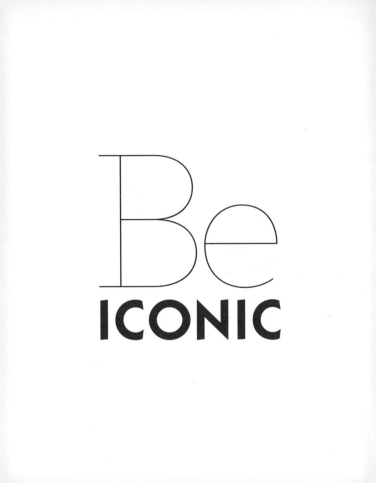

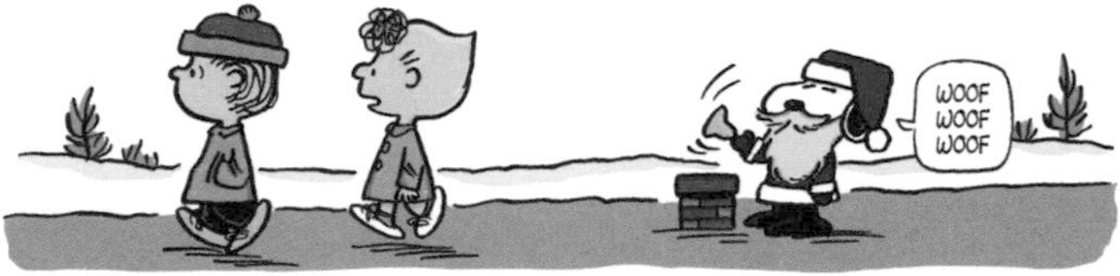
WOOF
WOOF
WOOF

"I thought Santa Claus said 'ho, ho, ho!'"

—*Sally*

Be
BLESSED

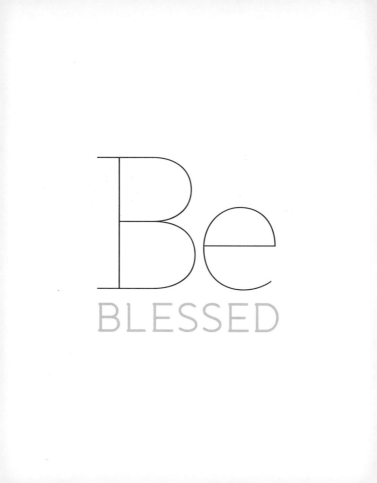

"Merry Christmas, little friend."

—*Snoopy*

Be
HEARD

"So the words spoken through Jeremiah the prophet were fulfilled: 'A voice was heard in Rama, wailing and loud laments; it was Rachel weeping for her children. And refusing all consolation because they were no more.' Matthew 2:17!"

—Linus

Be
Reflective

"Some dogs wait all day just for the opportunity to try to bite the mailman. I've never gone in much for that sort of thing. And I definitely would never even think of biting a mailman who was delivering Christmas cards!"

—*Snoopy*

Be
SWEET

Charlie Brown: Look what I got you for Christmas. A bowl full of chocolate chip cookies!

Snoopy: Wow!

Charlie Brown: I just hope you don't eat 'em all at once.

Be
FESTIVE

"Christmas decorations seem to be going up earlier every year."

—*Charlie Brown*

Be
Caring

Charlie Brown: It's bad enough that you two fight every day, but don't you realize what Santa Claus must think of you when you fight and argue this time of year?

Lucy: Dear brother!

Linus: Dear sister!

Be
CREATIVE

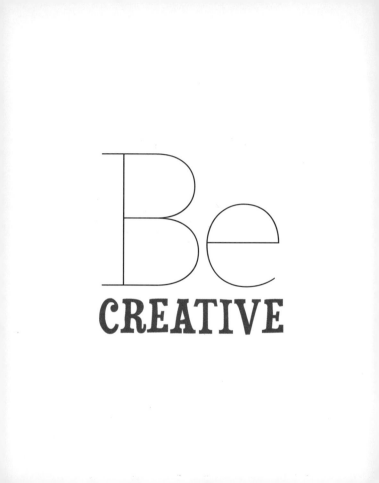

"The world is filled with comedians!"

—*Snoopy*

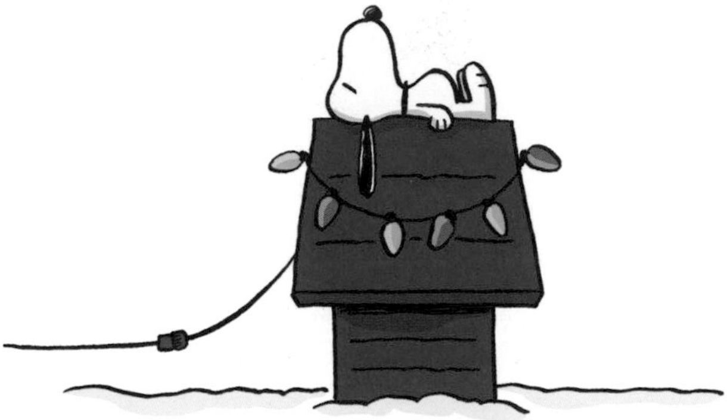

Be

Bright

Be
READY

Be
SMILEY

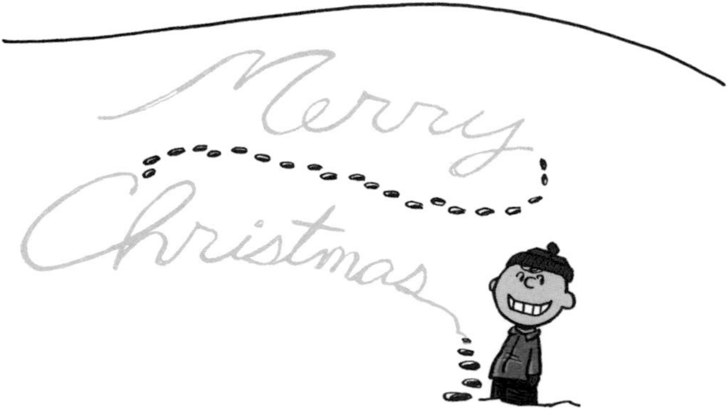
Merry Christmas

Be
Hopeful

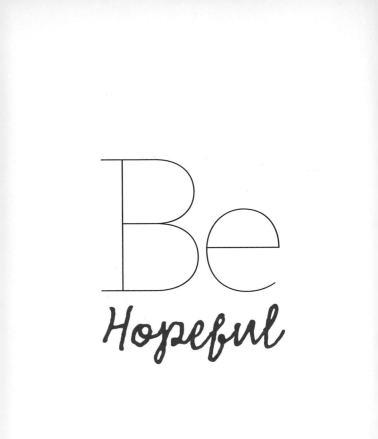

Lucy: I just noticed something about this room.

Schroeder: What's that?

Lucy: There's an appalling lack of mistletoe.

Be
RESTED

Be

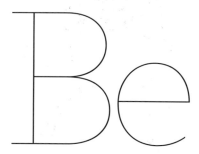

HEARTWARMING

Lucy: Rerun, as your big sister, I feel it is my duty to tell you that what you see is not the real Santa Claus. What you're looking at is a dog in a Santa Claus suit. Now that I've told you this, how does it make you feel?

Rerun: I like him!

Be
GIVING

"It's a new nest. Merry Christmas!"

—*Snoopy*

Be
AMAZED

"Happiness is a thoughtful friend."

—*Snoopy*

Be
Thoughtful

Peppermint Patty: Got any extra Christmas cards? I forgot to buy some. And how about stamps? I'll need some stamps, too. Here, keep this one. Then I won't have to send it to you.

Marcie: It's good to see you filled with the holiday spirit, sir.

Peppermint Patty: 'Tis the season to be sarcastic.

Be
JOLLY

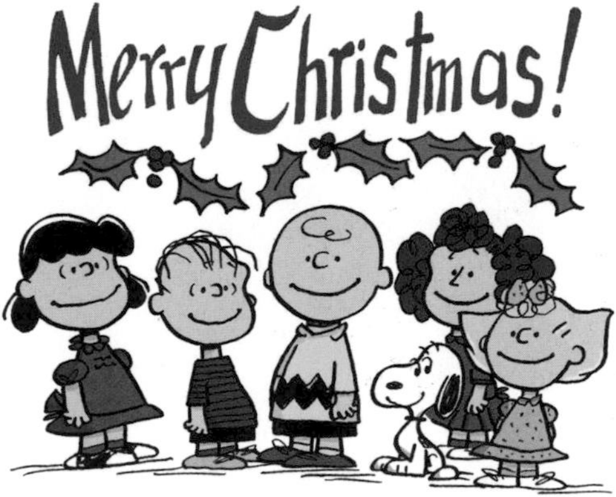
Merry Christmas!

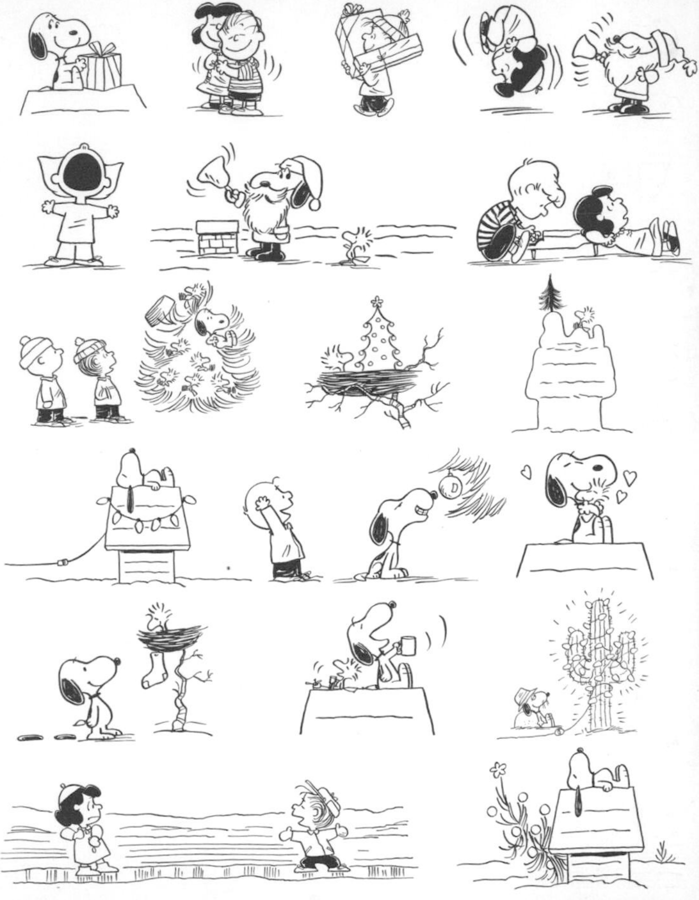